Remind Me Again

Jade Scorpion

This is a work of fiction. Names, characters, places, and incidents either are the product of the author's imagination or are used fictitiously.

Copyright © 2020 by Jade Scorpion

Cover Imaging/Design: Celina Burney

To my beautiful sisters

My darlings, I am so proud of the things you are accomplishing! Never stop reaching for the stars and trusting God! Always remember you can do anything you put your mind to, a and I have your back forever!

I Love You!

5

<u>Jasmine</u>

Apparently …

I have romanticized
This elaborate idea
That maybe
We could be the perfect family
It seemed so unfair
this bump in the road
had to define our destiny
But who am I
To think things would change
Everything exploded within a millisecond
Honestly, I am exhausted
With it all

Tireless

I have exhausted every emotion
I end my nights
Sitting in this dark room
Staring at the walls
Attempting to make sense
Of it all
Jane is up endless nights
Caring for these kids

She has never even given birth
I wonder most nights
How does she process this life?
With no visible anger
I'm almost sure
She's hurt
… Or angry
… Or furious
Something besides
This straight-faced emotion
We always see

Wandering

I look deep
    Into her eyes
        It is almost as if her soul aches
        I mean

It makes sense
    Your mom is in love
        With this man
Who clearly isn't your father

Your dad left
    Now suddenly, you are alone
        With a sister on the way
            And a mom whose focus
                No longer exists

Forget You

Slamming doors

"HOW COULD YOU?!"

"To think I believed you really loved me ... "

"Love you? ... I did until you left us all for
Charlie"

I guess this is it

The end of the road

He returned to leave once more
Staring into those big blue eyes

Oblivious

Blinded
By this timeless love
We share endless memories
But who cares
Clearly
She does not
I mean seriously
She traded us all
She has this thing for Charlie
She just can't seem to kick
Charlie awakened her inner beast

Charlie

She sold her soul
For the love of men
For a high
She would never reach again
She left us there
Anticipating a moment
The one where she would decide
to be our mother once more
But Charlie had her gone
She was addicted to the feel
All the late nights
Staggering in smiling
Like she couldn't feel her face
Eyes so glassy
You would think she could see the future
A monster
She would become
Without her lover
Charlie

Now let us press fast forward

Figuring It Out

Just the four of us now
    On our own
15 ... 11 ... 4 ... 1
    Jane has no choice but to play mom
But that is far from fair to her
    She has been at this
For quite some time now
    She has never had the chance to be a kid
Changing diapers
    Cooking dinner
Cleaning house
    Checking homework
She is only but 15 years old
    She begged mom to do right
But it went unheard
    If she wasn't sleeping it off
She was higher than the skies could reach

Jane

Understand

"Baby listen ...
Mama will get it right this time "
She would say
Empty words
To empty promises

She always got their hopes up
But you see
I knew better
Late nights
At grandma's

Mom could never
And I mean ever
Stay away long enough
To love us right
I was only 5
Jasmine was 1

And it was just us two
So, Grandma could handle us
Just fine

These Years

We have spent with Grandma
Have been the best ones yet
For us girls that is
But
I can see it in her eyes
The pain gets worse
As the years pass
Knowing her baby girl
Is in love with the "Devil"
As Granny says
She just can't fathom
How she could do this
To herself
To her mother
To her marriage

Most of all her children

What Now?

Grandma passed just last night
They say it was her heart
I mean
Watching your only daughter
Fall in love
With a monster
Especially one like Charlie
You are bound to fall
Fall victim to a broken heart
One day ...

Making Jasmine 7

Another One

(eye roll)
Now look at her
Staggering down the isle
At her mother's funeral
None the less
Belly round as a basketball
Honey brown eyes
Glazed over
Like two fresh donuts
You would think she would do better
At least this time
She is so gone
She wouldn't even know what year it is

Ugh!

Family snickering

        Pointing

I'm just a kid

           What about me

  What about Jas

    What about this unborn baby

She probably

       Doesn't even know this

Who Is the Dad?...

           Tell me that

Where?

Grandma's sister was just too old
She couldn't take care of herself
Let alone take care of us
But they didn't know where to put us
Because if the state finds out
They'll snatch us away
 then separate us
They couldn't have that
So …
To Aunt Sarah's house
We went

I Hate It Here!

It's like an old folks' home in here
Imagine it
Old dusty couches
Big box TV in the corner
It probably doesn't even work

Wigs sitting on the dining table
Looking like they might start walking at any
second
Not to mention
There's this dirty glass
It sits on her nightstand
Holding her teeth
TEETH!
YAY!

Perfect place to be

I GUESS

He's Here

Mom had Jackson last night
Yes, that's his name
She just can't stay away from that J
Maybe because she's a Jennifer
Not a history lesson
Just a clarity session
The baby is here now
Aunt Sarah can't do a newborn
So home we go
That didn't last long
The smell of molding dentures
Was making me nauseous
Anyway

Jackson ... Then Charlie

Such a precious baby he is
Meanwhile
She can't wait to be discharged
She says Charlie is awaiting her return
Wow Mom Really?!?
Eyes of judgment I give her
I was crazy
To even hope
That maybe number three
Would make her change
But you see
Charlie means more to her
More than we ever will

Clean Days

I wouldn't want to
Make her seem as if
She's this big bad mom-ster
She's had her days
They usually don't last
More than a week
She can at least do that
Sometimes
She'll try not to love Charlie
The way she really does
She'll try to be a good mom
She'll try to act as if
We really mean more to her
More to her than Charlie really does

Fail

It's only after someone
Some stranger
Or some nosey neighbor
Calls the cops
Complaining
"those kids are in that house alone"
"I know she's never there"
So here comes the state
Now we must act
As if she's the perfect single mom
What can I say
She cleans up well

Time

Fast forward
Just a few years
Here I am 14
Raising two kids
And these guys
Oh … these guys
they're in and out
All day and night
Mom is always
Way too stoned to realize
That they all have
Those big brown eyes
Planted on me

She thinks

She turns them on

Creeps

She thinks
They have the hots for her

But the reality is
Their eyes are
Dancing up my pretty brown thighs

Lustful thoughts
Lustful wishes

While she's dancing around
In those little white shorts
Higher than the skies can reach

Their eyes are gliding down my skin
Like its butter

They're only here
For her to get high

I must suffer
Just for her high

Scales

His hands feel like
           The scales of a snake
                      Scraping against my skin
                                 She's so high
                                      She's
              asleep on the couch
                         As always
Once she closed her eyes
            He crept in the kitchen
                        Just as I was making a bottle
                                   I could feel his hot breath
on my neck
                                            I felt a drop
of sweat on my shoulder
                              As he leaned in to whisper
Nasty nothings in my ear
              I was so disgusted
                   I sent him packing
                         With an ache between his
legs
                                   As his snake like
hands
                                      Crept on
my baby soft skin

The power behind my foot put him in shock

Why?

I have spent
A many days and nights
Trying to figure out
Why
Just why
She loves Charlie so much
You'd think
Having kids would change that
But it's like the moment
We come out
It's Charlie
In full force

Lustful Love

She's so in love
I can smell him
All over her skin
It's like his scent
Oozes from her pores
It's like watching a tornado form
With the first hit
She's sucking all the oxygen
From the room
She becomes so toxic
She becomes so absent

Dad

He left
When I was about 3
He loved mom
For as long as he could
But once again
She loved Charlie more
They had been together
For quite sometime
High school sweethearts
They loved each other so
But one day
Mom just couldn't handle
The stress became too much
Working a steady job
Being a wife
A mother to a toddler
She just couldn't handle

The Fall

She was holding on
Until one day
A coworker introduced her to
Charlie
It seemed to be love at first sight
When it began
Dad couldn't see the difference
Until she was out late nights
Spacey while she was home
Just not in tune
Charlie had taken over
She fell for him
So fast
No one saw it coming

Within

Like Eve in the garden
She took a bite
Of what seemed to be
Pure paradise
Sin in its most glorifying bliss
She had fallen for the trap
Once more
The snake in her garden
So skilled at persuasion
Convinced her that maybe
Just maybe
This was her destiny
She knew Charlie
Could never let her down
She'd found peace
With her new found destiny
She never saw it as defeat
As we all did

Good Night

Dad came around again
When I was about 10
To his surprise
There stood two little girls
With his big blue eyes
Took a swing
At that love thing again
But he struck out worse
Much worse than the first time
He swore he loved us both
With a kiss on the forehead
He left late one night

How?

I know what you're thinking
How could he
Not have known
How could he
Leave his pregnant wife
How could he
Leave her with a toddler to raise
He left her all alone

You don' t have to get it
But she was so spaced out
He didn't know who she was
Most days
She'd stagger in from work
Looking like a zombie
And he just couldn't figure out why

Jasmine

She was the kid he didn't know about
Mom found out she was pregnant
Right after he left
She searched
Day and night
It was probably more about Charlie than it was dad
Nonetheless she was looking
But it was as if he'd fallen from the Earth
This only made things worse
A single mom
A toddler
One on the way

dUmb

And then there's Charlie
He drives her crazy
She tried
Her entire pregnancy
But being without him
Was too hard for her
I could tell the nights
She would sneak him in
I guess she thought
I wouldn't notice
But I could tell
Just when
My mom wasn't focused

Mom

Jennifer

It was as if my life changed
All in one night
When I experienced Charlie
That first time
Was unexplainable
I mean it was the first time
It's always that first high
It felt like chasing a toddler
Down a never-ending hallway

I was searching once more
For that very first high
Every time I took a hit
Like Charlie and I had never met
I just can't seem to find that feeling again
So now I never want to come down
Maybe
Just maybe
If I build on it
I might just get there

Hi, my name is Jennifer
And I'm an addict

Rehab

I mean what did you think

Thought I never tried rehab huh
You thought I never tried to stop

I wanted to stop for my family
Especially my beautiful girls

I've gone to the NA meetings
I even tried quitting cold turkey

It was like my body
Took the most extreme changes
Like ...
Going from the center of the North Pole
At the dead of Winter
To the very pits of hell
The detox hurt too bad

I just had to take Charlie back

Sin

It's just too easy
To live a life
Full of sin
It seems so hard
to do the right thing
Be the perfect wife
An even better mom
Work a full-time job
Living a life
Without Charlie
Seemed to be so impossible
At least for me
It got me through the days
It was even better at night

Tears

The baby could cry all night
It wouldn't phase me
Not one bit
I would be so high
It suppressed every sound

My husband's rants
Seemed to fade in the distance
As if his mouth was moving
But no words would escape

Pregnant...AGAIN!!

It's like a rodeo
One man out
Another one in
Most days
I wish Jake never left
At least the kids would all have the same parents
At least the babies
Would have a chance at meeting their dad

I probably couldn't tell you who he is
When it means not having to deal
Deal with my true reality
I will do anything
I'm sure you knew this was coming

Silence

The silence seems to be so loud

Four walls

I'm trying to do it right this time
Trying to do better for this kid

Detoxing

During pregnancy

The hardest thing I've done

HELP

I'm crashing
Month 7
Not much longer
They say the baby is healthy
They say the baby will be fine
But only by the grace of God
Because these days
I simply can't be without him
With no remorse
The damage he could be doing to my child
I just simply can't let him go

46

<u>Goodbye</u>

She's Gone Now

I guess her heart
Just couldn't take anymore
She slipped away
Right after Jason was born
It was as if a sudden peace
Came over her
In that moment
I knew...
This is it
Charlie finally won

Mom passed last night
Now where do we go from here?
Remind me again
Why this life of sin
Was so important
The doctors say
It was simply too late
Charlie had taken her heart
Long before she closed her eyes
Remind me again
Why this life of sin
Was so important

9 798655 242951